SOMETHING CALLED MAGIC

Something Called Magic

TAYLOR COBLENTZ

Taylor\Coblentz

To my best friends in elementary school and our imaginary Time Warp game. Gabe, Lexi, and Kelsey—thank you for your young imaginations and friendship. Almost twenty years later, I finally finished the story we began so long ago.

Another special thank you to my mother and forever editor—Diane Cieslak.

Lastly, but certainly not least, thank you to Brooke Hitchcock-Montoya for the beautiful cover and support. I am incredibly blessed by your friendship and your talent.

Chapter One

Christal

BINGGGG! My head collided with the silver metal pole of the monkey bar. I jolted backwards, trying not to fall into the mud, as the stars in my eyes twinkled like the night sky. Jess asked if I was okay, while my other two sisters stumbled on through the mucky field, not even noticing my minor accident.

"Yeah, I am fine. I just hope that I won't have a swollen bump on my head at school tomorrow! That'd be a fun one to have to explain," I said giggling, as I rubbed my sore forehead and tried to regain my balance. My eyes were only watering a little.

"Yeah, 'Hi Mrs. McGrady, I hit my head on a pole while staring at the boys walking home,'" Jess said giggling while she mocked me.

"I was *not!*" I quickly responded. How embarrassing—I hoped no one else saw.

My three sisters and I were heading home from

school through the upper elementary playground. We walked home every day because we lived so close. A perfect view of our house could be seen through a set of trees right next to the recess area. We were lucky to be able to walk to school every day, even though it didn't always feel like it during the winter months in Michigan. Jess and I trotted to catch up with Kate and Izzy, my other two sisters.

Nearing our backyard, I admired our new in-ground pool and the wooden tree house our father had built us about a year before. My dad claims that he built it to make us happy, but if you ask me, I think he just wanted a place we could go in order to give him some peace and quiet in the house! We could climb a five-foot ladder to reach the entryway of the tree house that sat between two huge trees in our yard. It was just large enough for all of us to sit criss-cross-applesauce in a circle. We spent so much time talking and laughing together in there.

I was so glad the weather was finally warming up enough to be outside and in the pool again. It was getting closer and closer to summer vacation, when my sisters and I would be able to hang out every day from dawn to dusk. Dad was planning on opening the pool soon, so we would finally be able to get back to one of our favorite pastimes. It had felt like a long winter.

Weren't we so lucky that our parents had four girls so close in age? Kate and Jess were fraternal twins born the year after me. They were finishing up the fifth grade. Izzy came a year later and was just finishing fourth grade. Then there was our sweet baby sister, Lucy. I think my dad wanted a boy if I am being honest... but us girls just kept coming!

We walked around the side of the house to get to our front door. I ran up the front steps and opened the door with my "royal key." My parents always left me in charge since I was in sixth grade and would be in middle school after the upcoming summer passed. I twisted and turned the gold key until the door opened with a slight creak.

Izzy scurried in before I could even open the door all the way. She went into the kitchen to check voice-mail messages on our home phone's answering ma-chine, like always. Yes, we still had a home phone with an answering machine. None of us had cell phones yet (trust me—we tried), so that was my parent's best solution.

Anyways, that was the daily routine. Our parents usually worked until 5:30, so after school let out around 3:00, we were on our own for a few hours. Our father was a doctor at a local hospital and our mother was a veterinarian. They were two of the nicest people in the entire country, always caring for someone or something else more than themselves. In fact, even when they'd come home from work, they'd still have five kids to attend to, and we usually acted like the animals that Mom took care of during the day.

I went inside our house, flipped off my white sneak-ers that were now coated in mud, and sock-glided into the kitchen next to Izzy. Jess pounded up the stairs to start getting ready for her soccer practice. I could hear the wood creaking upstairs as she frantically moved around looking for clean clothes. Kate, of course, immediately went to do her homework up in her bedroom. Mom claimed that Kate had been reading and writing since the day she was born!

Izzy pressed the blinking red button on the voicemail machine and the first message began. It was just a message from some telemarketer. Now that everyone else in the world had cell phones, we usually only had calls coming in from telemarketers or our parents.

Izzy immediately deleted that message, keeping her finger near the delete button in preparation for the next spam voicemail.

If only we had known what was *actually* waiting for us.

Chapter Two

Christal

"Hi girls, this is Mom. Just wanted to let you know that your father and I got out of work early and went out to get groceries together with Lucy. We will be home... watch out honey! I love..." The words ended abruptly as the phone went silent, and with a beep, the message concluded. Izzy and I stood there staring at each other, not knowing what had just happened.

As I looked into Izzy's eyes, I saw tears running down her pink cheeks, as my own eyes started to blur. I dropped down to the brown hardwood floor with a thump. Why had mom's call ended so abruptly? Why was she trying to say that she loved us before the message ended? Why hadn't she called back since then? There were no more messages.

"Okay, I am leaving for soccer now! I want to get there a little early to practice on the field. Do you know if we have any more water bottles in the garage?" Jess asked as she came leaping down the stairs wearing her soccer shorts and practice jersey. She looked over at Izzy and me with her shiny brown eyes when we didn't respond. "What's wrong?" she asked, immediately running over to the both of us, noticing that we were crumbling into pieces. I shakily pointed to the answering-machine without saying a word. Jess played the message but didn't react. She stared blankly at the machine in horror. "You guys don't think that... well you know... something actually happened to them, do you?" Jess finally asked with a lump in her throat.

"I don't know. I don't know what to think right now Jess," I choked out. "But I do know that we should go get Kate, cause it doesn't seem good."

I stood up slowly, shaking from all the terrible thoughts I couldn't push out of my head. My parents had always told me to take care of my younger sisters; yet, at a time that I needed to, I didn't feel able. I was, of course, thinking the worst as we went up the stairs to tell Kate.

I knocked quietly on the door to her room before pushing it open. "Ugh, you guys know this is my study time; what are you doing up here?" Kate asked when she heard our footsteps. She was still staring down at her math workbook in deep concentration.

"Kate. It's important," I said, and she alarmingly turned around in her chair when she heard the fear in my voice. I instantly saw her facial expression change from an annoyed cringe to a look of dread, her eyes widening with concern.

"Mom and Dad were out getting groceries with Lucy. Mom left us a voicemail, but the message ended with what sounded like a car crash. Mom sounded really panicked before it ended. We're not sure, but we can't help but think the worst has happened," I could barely get all my words out without breaking down again.

Kate stood up without giving any clear facial response to what I had just told her. Eventually, after moments of silence, Kate said, "We should probably try calling them back, don't you think?" Perhaps we were just being dramatic. Everything could be completely fine. Maybe Mom's phone just died.

We all agreed and headed back downstairs to our living room. Izzy tried calling both Mom's and Dad's cell phones, but neither one answered and instead went straight to voicemail like the phones were off. We were used to our parents not answering during the day, like when they were in surgery or something, but after work, we were always a priority that they never ignored.

While Izzy continued to repeatedly call our parents' phones, Kate turned on the TV to see if anything on the news mentioned our parents. Although the local news did not directly feature our parents, the overly made-up reporter did broadcast several accidents that had recently occurred, one of them fatal. She solemnly identified the un-named victims as an adult female, an adult male, and a small infant. The reporter couldn't share any identifying details other than the fact that all three victims died on impact. The driver of the car that hit them survived, but was in critical condition.

The worry and heartache became too much for me to handle, so I ran out the back sliding door. I needed some fresh air, and a chance to gather my thoughts. My head was brutally banging like a drum from a combination of the shock and my run-in with the pole earlier.

Walking as fast as I could, I went into our back-yard and headed towards our school's playground. I had a favorite spot where I always liked to go when I was upset or needed to think. My little spot was right under two willow trees, where there was a perfect area hidden by the branches and wispy layers of greenery. I sat down on one of the thick logs that I had formerly placed there, and took a deep, unstable breath. My hands were shaking like the leaves in the tree above me. How could this be happening? This had to be a nightmare, right?

After a few brief moments, I heard a whisper. I looked around to see if one of my sister's had followed me, but saw no one near me. Again, another whisper, "Stop! You're stepping on me! Move over there!" I wondered if it could just be my imagination running wild, but the voice seemed too real.

"Shh! She will hear you!" another voice said. Just then, a large book dropped from the tree. "Oops..." the voice said immediately. I looked up into the tree but could not see anything but the leaves adjusting to the movement of the book. The heavy book scattered the dirt on the ground as it collided with the earth's surface. The book, along with my socks, had also become covered with dry dirt. I hesitantly picked it up and blew off some of the earthly dust before standing to get a better look up into the tree. I tried peeking through the branches.

"Hello? Is someone up there?" I asked, speaking to the branches towering over my head. "Please come down if you are. Do you need this book?"

I looked down at the book in my hands. It was dark brown with a hard cover. It had nothing written on the front, or the back, or the spine. At first, I thought it might be a dictionary. Who uses those anymore though?

Glancing up into the branches again, I still could not see anything. It was so strange. I was about to run back to the safety of my house, fearing the worst, but my curiosity got the best of me.

Chapter Three

Christal

There was a picture in the book. Not just any picture. It was a picture of our parents and Lucy. A recent picture I had never seen before.

I couldn't believe it. What in the world was going on? Why did this book fall from the sky and have a picture of my parents and baby sister?

I quickly flipped to the next page, anxious to see what else was in this mysterious book. It had pictures of rings on one page. Each ring had descriptions including special powers that someone could use on an "adventure" that the book kept referencing. It was then that I noticed a small paragraph in the corner of the page:

Izzy, Kate, Christal, and Jess,

It is your job to save the lives of the ones you love the most. Don't be afraid, for you have each other. Love, after all, is the greatest power one can ever have. Good luck on your journey.

This book was clearly created just for us. I was so confused and couldn't deal with this alone any longer. I started toward the house to get my sisters when I heard another large plop behind me. I nearly jumped a mile.

"It's okay to be scared," a spunky little voice chirped from a girl that I had now turned around to see. She appeared to be a young adult, but was very tiny with unusually petite facial features. "Go get your sisters darling and bring them back here. I will explain every-thing once you return," she said with a shy smile.

I nodded, not sure what else to do. This was just plain... strange! I gently set the book on the ground and sprinted faster than an Olympian to the back sliding door of my house. My lungs were on fire by the time I opened the door and yelled for my sisters to quickly come outside. I didn't have time to give them an explanation. I just told them to come with me. They followed me out to the trees, clearly confused and anxious, looking at me like I was crazy.

When we reached the spot where I had placed the

book under the trees, there was another girl there with the one who had spoken to me. My sisters and I cautiously approached them, panting like dogs from the sprint and exhilaration. This felt like a "stranger danger" situation.

"Hi! I am Amanda!" the girl that had previously spoken to me said. This time she gave us a smile that took up nearly half of her face.

"I'm Anne. We are *very* sorry about your parents' and little sister's deaths," said the other, abruptly bringing to light what we had all feared was true. I looked around to find that tears were quickly pooling in my sisters' eyes again—if they had ever even stopped.

Anne had a calmness about her. Her voice gently echoed in the air and her petite features made her look so innocent. She also came across as more mature and in control.

Together, Anne and Amanda looked like what I can only describe as fairies but were at least four feet tall. They wore shimmery pink and white dresses that flowed down the length of their small bodies. The sun glimmered upon them making them seem as if they were only a figment of our imaginations. They didn't have wings, but definitely were not from our ordinary world. Their voices, surprisingly, had a normal pitch; not like those tiny voices you hear in movies. Their facial features seemed unusual though, compared to ours. Their noses were as tiny as buttons, their cheeks were bright and rosy, and their large eyes seemed as if they could see the whole world in one glance. I wondered if they were twins, as they also looked identical. Maybe they were a mix of elf, fairy, and human?

"How do you know they died? Are you sure?" Kate questioned in disbelief, trying to breathe through a minor panic attack.

"My dear, Kate. We don't like burdening you with this heavy news. However, it is true. Your parents and Lucy were killed in a car accident," Anne said. I could see the tears glistening in Anne's eyes, telling me she really did feel sorry for us.

"We are here to help you. It's not too late to change your family's destiny if you work together," Anne explained.

"Oh. Let me give you these now," Amanda said. She held out her tiny palm and displayed four beautiful rings, each with a unique pattern and color. I recognized these rings from the picture I'd glanced at in the book minutes earlier.

"You will need these rings for the adventure you are about to take," Amanda continued and we all immediately nodded our heads, still in shock. "Come on, put them on! There's one for each of you!" Amanda said as she tiptoed around enthusiastically, placing a ring in each of our open palms. Amanda definitely had one of those shining personalities that could brighten even the darkest room. She somehow brought hope and zeal into the toughest of moments.

I placed the ring she gave me on the ring finger of my right hand, not sure what to expect. Nothing happened. I waited, and waited, and still nothing happened. I examined my ring closely. It was white with pink swirls moving through it like an electric current. I had never seen such an incredible piece of jewelry. My mom had some stunning and shimmery diamond pieces, but it wasn't even comparable.

As far as I could see, Izzy's ring was white with purple swirls moving through it just like mine. Similarly, Jess' and Kate's ring had the same appearance, except Jess' swirls were orange, and Kate's were blue.

"They don't seem to be working," Izzy said with a frown.

"You don't even know what should happen my dear," Amanda responded in the same tone that a teacher uses when her students are being impatient.

"Well, nothing's happening," Izzy mumbled under her breath. She had quite the attitude when she wanted one.

"The rings' powers are only to be used when they are needed on your adventure. Everything you will need to know about them will be in the book we have given you. We wish you the best of luck," Anne said with a wink. In the next instant, she and Amanda were gone.

I had never in my short life been through such a strange encounter. I couldn't help but wonder if it was actually real or if anxiety and stress had taken over my mind. Not to mention, I had so many questions to ask those fairy-like girls, and they just vanished into thin air!

"That was weird, but whether they work or not we at least have these gorgeous rings!" Izzy said being her normal peppy self and breaking the silence. Kate, Jess, and I all just shrugged and gently smiled at our silly sister. She always tried to make the best of any situation, but unfortunately, I wasn't in the mood for laughter. Especially if we were to believe our parents and sister were dead. My eyes felt droopy from being overwhelmed with tears and the heaviness in my chest weighed me down. The sick feeling carried into my stomach, making me feel like I could throw up any second.

Despite wanting to lay on the ground and cry, I lifted the book from the ground where I had dropped it and began to skim through more of the pages. "Look! Here's a page about the rings. This is the book that Anne and Amanda left here for us."

The girls gathered around me, trying to get the best view of the page.

For the eldest: This white and pink ring gives the power to transform.

For the most timid: This white and orange ring gives the power to create fire, wind, ice, and water.

For the most outgoing: This white and purple ring gives the power to fast forward or slow down small amounts of time.

For the most wise: This white and blue ring gives the power to read others' thoughts.

How could this book know so much? It was like a book version of Kate's brain. Though I was slightly disappointed that I wasn't labeled the "most wise," I understood why in comparison to Kate.

A few minutes later, I grabbed the heavy book and we headed speechlessly into the house. Once inside, Kate asked me for the book and began reading through it. She found another page about the rings, one with directions. It was just what we needed.

1. *Put the ring on the pointer finger of your right hand.*

2. *Think about the ones you love most.*

That was all. I switched the ring to my pointer finger and was surprised at how it still fit snugly. I thought about my sisters first and then about my parents and how much I loved them. My sisters looked like they were doing the same thing by the way they were staring deeply into their rings. I would've done anything to get my parents and Lucy back.

* * *

I am convinced that I will never see anything so beautiful again. Suddenly, before my eyes, a large whirlwind of colors appeared, circling and looping through one another in zaps of bright intensity. I couldn't take my eyes off it. My sisters were seeing the same thing. The colors intrigued and enchanted all of us. Finally, Kate spoke up, "The book tells us to walk into it." Okay. Kate was smart, but she must have read that wrong somehow.

"What do you mean? Why would we want to do that?" I asked.

"The book calls it a Time Warp. We have to enter it in order to go on this adventure that it keeps referring to," Kate replied.

I nodded in response to Kate's explanation. I knew that we had to move quickly, believing that our parents really were gone. It was only a matter of time before the police would figure out that they had other children at home. Someone, either from child welfare services or a family member would be coming to get us soon, so we needed to move fast and get out of there if we were going to go save them somehow. There were so many unknowns, but we had to take the chance, especially if it gave us any hope of getting our parents and sister back.

Once I realized I was still in my socks, I quickly put on some trusty tennis shoes. In hindsight, I wish I would have thought to bring a jacket too. I had no clue what to even be prepared for.

All I knew was that I had to go first. I'm the oldest,

and I wouldn't have it any other way. I would rather risk it myself than send one of my younger sisters into a crazy tunnel of whatever it was. I couldn't believe what I was about to do. None of this made any sense, and I was relying on the advice of two strange fairy girls to guide me into a pretty tunnel into the unknown. What was I thinking?

I inched closer to the Time Warp, each step escalating my fear, as if inching closer and closer to the edge of a cliff. Taking a long deep breath, I looked back at my sisters behind me with their raised eyebrows, puckered lips, and teary eyes. I could hear the wind roaring from within the Time Warp, drawing me in.

"You all have to follow me once I jump in, and please hurry. Wherever this takes me, I don't want to be alone for long," I said. "Kate, you'll bring the book, right?"

"Already planned on it, Sis! We will be right behind you," Kate responded.

With her words, I closed my eyes and stepped forward into the endless swirl of colors.

Chapter Four

Kate

Just like that, Christal was gone. She basically jumped forward and disappeared into thin air.

Now, I have read a lot of books. None of them ever mentioned anything like this. I have read fiction, non-fiction, fantasy, comics, and everything in between, but none would help me understand what in the world was going on. Of course, the idea of time travel was as old as time. But did I think it actually existed? Definitely not.

Either way, I did not like the feeling of helplessness. I would have preferred to be prepared and know what I was doing. It was like walking into class to take a test without having studied at all. Just wasn't something I felt comfortable with.

Though I was beginning to second guess our decision to jump into the Time Warp, I was not about to leave Christal floating alone wherever she ended up.

As I was tied for second oldest with Jess, I decided to go next. After snagging a small backpack to put the book in, I quietly stepped forward, waved hesitantly at my two other sisters, and jumped in feet first.

For what seemed like a whole minute, I was floating. I was watching the colors swirl and twirl around me endlessly, getting dizzier by the second. I could not see Christal ahead, and I could not see Jess or Izzy either, who I'd hoped followed me immediately. I imagined that this weightlessness was what it felt like to be up in space, minus all the colors.

I finally started to see and feel something that looked like reality. I could see bright green moss under my feet, and slowly the Time Warp began to fade away color by color until it was completely gone.

I widened my eyes to take in the full view of my new location. Christal was dusting herself off, as her landing had not been quite as pleasant. It looked like she had landed right in a pile of hard, dry, dusty dirt. I, on the other hand, had luckily landed gently on a patch of soft and squishy moss. I looked around as I caught my breath, realizing I had been holding it the whole time I was in the Time Warp. It reminded me of jumping off the high dive into a deep pool.

There were trees everywhere and birds chirping both close by and what seemed to be far away. The sun was peeking through the treetops, giving us enough light to see our surroundings. I noticed the tree vines connecting a vast jungle of plants that looked like a spider's web in every direction. Then, of course, I saw

Jess and Izzy tumbling onto the jungle floor nearly on top of one another. If this hadn't been such a serious situation, I would have been laughing my head off at the sight.

"We were too scared to go in alone, so we went at the same time!" Izzy explained after seeing my surprised expression at their close arrival.

All four of us took the time to wander around our nearby surroundings. We still had no idea why the Time Warp would drop us in the middle of a jungle. We had no clue where we were. We also had no clue how we were even here to begin with. All we knew was that we had powerful rings and a book to guide us. I needed to find out more.

Chapter Five

Kate

I sat down on a sturdy log nearby with the book to investigate a little further, while the others continued to walk around the close area. As the book was the size of a wide encyclopedia, it had to have plenty of information that we could use.

After speed reading for just a few minutes, I discovered more about what the purpose of the Time Warp was:

The Time Warp will take you where you need to go. But it won't take you there right away. Follow your hearts and fight with your love, and your destination will be your reward.

"What in the world..." I accidentally spoke aloud.

"Kate! What did you find?" Christal ran over, as Jess followed closely behind.

"I could be wrong, but I think...that the Time Warp will take us back to the time before Mom, Dad, and Lucy died," I said, barely believing my own words.

"That way, we would be able to stop them from going grocery shopping before the crash, and then they wouldn't die..." Christal continued my thoughts.

"I imagine that we need to keep traveling through the Time Warp until we make it to the right time period and place," I explained.

"Well, this definitely isn't it!" Izzy shouted, standing on top of a rock taller than all of us.

Chapter Six

Izzy

I am only ten years old, but people say I have the wit of a forty-year-old. I just like to lighten the mood and not take everything so seriously. Well, I mean, this was a serious situation. Extremely serious. Our parents' and Lucy's *lives* were on the line. I knew that. But, my sisters, especially Kate and Christal, could be so controlling. It's nice to add a little bit of fresh Izzy "air" sometimes.

"I think it's about time we go back in that weird thingy!" I told my sisters, as I jumped off the rock and skipped towards them. However, before they could reply, we were interrupted by a loud sound right behind us. It sounded like someone was sawing wood close by, but I wondered how that could be the case. We hadn't seen anyone in the nearby area.

Fearing for my life, I slowly turned my head to see

where it was coming from. Even though I knew that it might be coming from a source I wasn't going to like.

"That's a jaguar..." Kate whispered, just loud enough for me to hear. It was lingering about 30 feet in front of us, pacing back and forth. His bright eyes were glued to the four of us, standing out amongst his brown and yellow fur. I nervously started to pick at my fingernails, trying to think of something that we could do to escape this beast.

It was then that I noticed my ring again.

"We should just open the Time Warp up again and get out of here!" I suggested immediately. We all still had our rings on and began to think about our parents and Lucy. For some reason, the Time Warp wasn't appearing like it did before. We didn't have much time, and we couldn't wait around to figure out why the Time Warp wasn't working.

"Christal!" I whispered as loudly as I could to get her attention again. "Your power is to transform, isn't it?" She nodded. "Turn into something that could save us from this jaguar!"

I was proud of my ability to think quickly to come up with this plan, even though I did not know what type of animal would even be able to compete. A lot of animals could help us get away, but which one would be able to fit all of us on her back? Even better, what animal might the jaguar be afraid of?

Christal nodded, "Okay, but what animal would be good enough?"

"Kate, do they have any predators?" I asked.

"No...not that I remember at least," Kate answered, heightening my fears. I could tell by her tense facial expression that she was deep in thought. She always creased her eyebrows when she was brainstorming.

"What about a cheetah?" Jess quietly suggested. "They're even faster than a jaguar. Our soccer coach always tells us to run like a cheetah, especially when we play against the team named the Jaguars."

"Hmm. You're right about their speed, but I don't think all of us would be able to fit on one. That would be a little cruel to do to Christal," Kate answered, still in a hushed tone. The jaguar was still just pacing back and forth. It hadn't moved any closer, but it wasn't moving away either.

"What about an elephant?" Christal suggested. "It would be able to fit all three of you and I don't think a jaguar could attack it."

I watched Kate think for a second. "I think that's our best option right now. Christal, you ready?" Kate responded.

Christal looked a little like a deer in headlights. Even though the elephant was her idea, I could tell that she was as unsure about this as all of us. "I guess I have to be. Let's see how this goes."

Right before my eyes, Christal began to get taller, widen and grow large feet and gray skin. Though she had lost her ability to speak like a human, we knew the plan. She was nearly ten feet tall, so we hoisted and tugged one another up on her back as she kneeled on her front legs. She was at least eighteen feet long and thick like a brick. Even still, we squeezed together as close as possible so we could all fit and not fall off. As soon as we were safely on her back, holding onto each other with one hand and Christal's rough and wrinkly back with the other, we gave her a tap to tell her to bolt before the jaguar made its move.

She began to trot in the direction away from the jaguar. I felt like I was riding in a car with all the windows down, wishing I had a seat belt on. Mom always made me wear my seatbelt… now I knew why. We didn't have much to grab onto and I constantly felt like I was going to tumble off her back. Though elephants aren't crazy fast, Christal was able to move at a steady pace.

We continued through the forest with Christal hopping over fallen branches here and there. Each bounce left us holding on for dear life. Every time I looked behind us, hoping we had escaped, the jaguar was trailing just close enough to make us fearfully uncomfortable and very nervous.

I could tell that Christal was starting to get tired, as her pace slowed a bit. Fortunately, the jaguar seemed to be getting tired too. Though jaguars are twice as fast as elephants, our one saving grace was that the jaguar was only curiously lurking behind, rather than straight out sprinting towards us. Within the next few minutes, the jaguar gave up the hunt, and we were far enough ahead of it to be safe.

Once again, Christal kneeled on her front knees to let us carefully jump off her back. I stared at her huge trunk wagging back and forth like a dog's tail. It felt unreal that my sister was an elephant.

Seconds later, Christal transformed back into herself. We knew what we had to do, with no time to waste. Hopefully it would work this time.

Chapter Seven

Jess

The Time Warp, once again, did not take us where we needed to go. In fact, it seemed that this destination was actually a little worse. We were grateful it worked and had yet to figure out why it hadn't worked earlier when we needed it to, but this location was not what we had in mind.

I was plopped onto a sandy beach and Christal followed shortly after. We waited a few minutes, but Kate and Izzy didn't come. As I looked around at our beachy setting, I realized we were surrounded by water on what could only be a very small island. The island we were on wasn't much larger than a football field and there was nothing but sand and water—not even a single bit of vegetation for shade. I could see there was more land on the horizon, but it seemed like it was at least a mile away.

It was when I was staring at the distant land that

I noticed two very small figures wildly waving their hands back and forth in the air.

"Oh boy," Christal muttered, taking a deep breath, as she had just seen Kate and Izzy across the ocean as well.

"This is not good," I responded while squinting my eyes in the bright sun to see my other sisters.

"How did this even happen?" Christal wondered aloud.

I thought and thought about how I could possibly use my powers to help our current situation. We could not get back into the Time Warp because we did not know if it would take our sisters a totally different place and we could not risk being separated. It would be no help for Izzy to control time, and Kate wouldn't be able to read anyone's minds but ours. Christal could turn into an aquatic animal to swim us across but I don't think either of us were keen on getting into the deep, choppy, frigid water.

I stared deeply into my ring as I thought. The book said that I could create fire, water, wind, and ice... that's it! Ice! If I could freeze the water, we could easily walk across to Kate and Izzy!

"Christal, I have an idea... I am going to freeze the water so we can get across!" I don't think I had ever been so confident, and in a way, bossy. I have always been that one girl playing the flute in the background, and at that moment, I felt like the conductor of a symphony.

Christal just nodded quickly, accepting the idea

with no argument. I closed my eyes and thought about my parents. Then, when I opened them, beautiful crystals started to form on the water's surface. The water in front of us became white ice that shimmered in the brilliant sunrays like diamonds. The temperature cooled, despite the warmth radiating from the sun. I began to shiver with little goosebumps starting to cover my forearms and legs. Ice surrounded us on all sides, but I could see where it ended. My powers could only be so strong, and I imagine an entire ocean would take a lot of magic to freeze. We had to assume the ice went far enough to make it to our sisters at least.

We immediately started across the icy ocean toward our other half. Now, this was not a short sprint by any means. I don't think my soccer practices had prepared me for the sort of endurance I needed to cross a mile or so of ice. My tennis shoes kept slipping out from under me, nearly causing me to tumble with each stride. I could hear the crinkle and crackle of ice behind my every step, knowing that I was one small slip away from falling through the ice into the deep ocean.

And then I did.

* * *

My knee slammed to the ice as I lost my balance, and the force was too much for the ice to bear. It popped a hole right through the ice, so my whole leg fell directly into the freezing cold water. The current pulled me in like quicksand until only my head was above water. My arms flailed and struggled to hold onto bits and pieces of ice around me that just kept breaking away. My knee ached like it had been sliced into two pieces by a saw. I couldn't tell if it was broken, bleeding, or just bruised; but at this moment, it didn't really matter. I just had to live.

In brief and frantic glances, I could see Christal panicking on the solid ice just five feet away from me. She was screaming my name. "Jess! Jess! You need to create water. Create water!"

I had no clue how creating water would help, but I did not give myself time to think it through either. I trusted Christal and I was too cold and frantic to think straight.

Water shot up from under me, sending me flying headfirst into the blue sky. I was terrified, having no idea how I would ever make a safe landing. As I was descending to what could only be a hard, tough arrival on the ice, a huge white bird came swooping up from under me, guiding me right onto its' back. I had never heard of such a large, strong, incredible bird. I had no time to question my good fortune as I held on tightly to its feathers while the bird flew me over to where Kate and Izzy were standing on the land.

It was then that I wondered where Christal was. Was she still back on the ice where I had fallen in? Had she fallen in too?

My questions were answered as the four-foot-tall

bird, now standing on the sand next to my sisters, morphed into a very human, Christal.

"Why did we not think of a bird before, instead of the ice?" Christal exclaimed as she immediately hugged me. "I was so scared!"

"What type of bird was that? I have never seen one that large in my life," I responded, still in shock and breathing heavily from a combination of nerves and icy water. I laid down on my back and just tried to catch my breath after all the exhilaration. I was exhausted, and not to mention, very, very wet and cold. So much for not getting in the water.

"It was a Haast eagle. They are extinct now, so I had to hope that we were in a time period when they existed or that the magic didn't limit itself to current time periods. I read about them in a science book my teacher gave me."

"I am kind of afraid to ask... how long ago did they exist?" I asked, hesitant to learn how far back in time we were.

"They went extinct around the 1400s I think," Christal said. "For real though, you terrified me Jess. You gave me like, five seconds to think of a plan."

"Yeah, thank you for that. Let's stick with all your plans from now on please." I no longer wanted to be the conductor and was quite okay with being a flute player in the way, way back.

My sisters laid down next to me on the beach to help keep me warm while I dried off in the sun. We all needed time to calm down and relax for a few minutes. It felt like one of those moments when you really, really need a nap and can barely keep your eyes open. I also just felt like crying. Though we had not been going through the Time Warp for very long, it had already taken a toll on our bodies *and* hearts.

Chapter Eight

Jess

"So how did it feel to be an elephant and a bird?" Izzy asked as we laid on the beach. We all busted out laughing.

"I honestly don't even think I can describe the feeling. My nose felt huge as an elephant and as an eagle I was terrified that if I stopped frantically flapping my wings that I would fall into the ocean," Christal said.

"You have the coolest power I think," Izzy responded.

"Maybe. I think Kate's power to read minds is pretty cool. Then I could find out all of your secrets!" Christal smirked and purposefully laughed like an evil vampire.

"Who knows, maybe I've already done that!" Kate teased.

* * *

Christal thought we should look through the book a little more before making another move, so we sat up and planted our bottoms in the sand in a kindergarten carpet style circle. The midday sun was now shining on the shoreline, leaving a peaceful reflection on the calm water and warming the sand to a perfect toasty degree.

"I have sand everywhere, even in my pants!" Izzy said as she sat down. She was wearing short jean shorts, so I could understand her problem. She always cracked me up.

Kate had been holding onto the book in a small brown backpack from home, so she took it out and laid it in the patch of sand in the middle of our circle. We reviewed the first few pages again and then dug deeper into the book. One page told us a little more about the purpose of our journey.

When you lose someone you love, you don't always get a second chance to save them. This time, you do. Don't give up on the people most important to you.

Another page was a little less helpful. Or was it?

*Singing while in the Time Warp helps with the
nausea and will also make the time pass more
quickly.*

The page then proceeded to suggest some songs to
sing. Izzy was the only one who found this amusing.
She could and *would* sing everything, whether it was a
new top hit or the alphabet song.

"Can we look for anything the book says about why
the Time Warp didn't open up earlier?" Christal asked
the group. "It would just be nice to know in case
something like that happens again."

Kate nodded and began to flip through some more
pages. She came across a section about the Time Warp
and her eyes scanned quickly through the words.

"Ah! Here's something. So, the book says the Time
Warp needs a sort of 'break' in between use. It doesn't
give an exact time, but says that it can't be used again
right away," Kate said.

"That makes sense. We had probably only been
there ten minutes or so. That must be too soon,"
Christal responded.

Eventually we closed the book. We figured we
should explore our surroundings for any type of food.
Though we had traveled through many years of time,
it was only just getting close to our regular dinner
time. Our stomachs knew the time, even when a watch
didn't. We knew that we would have to eat at some
point and finding food probably wouldn't be easy.

We traveled a little deeper into the surrounding land, but found nothing but plushy trees, bushes, and streaming water. None of us knew enough about plants that we could risk trying something new in the wilderness. Christal considered trying to catch a fish with her bare hands, Izzy proposed that Christal could turn into a chicken to lay eggs that we could eat, and Kate couldn't think of anything but didn't think that either of those plans would work.

So, we decided that we had to move on, hoping that there would be better opportunities for food at our next destination. We held hands and thought of our parents. Then came that beautiful Time Warp! This time, we all jumped in at the exact same time to avoid more problems.

Chapter Nine

Izzy

Why does this Time Warp thing have to be so hard? I am not saying it's supposed to be easy, but it's just that, you know, we either go too far into the past or too far into the future. However, at least this was a much softer landing than the last few times. We plopped down on a neon orange couch that had large pink polka dots. Compared to our last few landings, this one seemed much more normal, despite the unusual cloth couch that looked like it came from a cartoon. It was cozy, but the design was a bit tacky.

We were just in a house. I did not see anyone else there but us. In fact, the house looked like it had never been lived in. The wood floors were so clean that they gleamed. The walls were freshly painted yellow and perfectly spotless without dents or black scuff marks from soccer balls hitting them. There were more windows than walls though, and through the large windows I could clearly see that it was dark outside except for the glow from city building lights in the short distance.

I stood up and headed straight through the doorway to the kitchen. I opened the fridge to discover fresh fruits, vegetables, sandwich meat, and cheese filling the shelves. With excitement, I then opened cupboards, finding more and more food like fresh sourdough bread and soft chocolate chip cookies. "Man, I am glad we didn't catch our own fish!" I hollered to my sisters. They cowered in the doorway looking at me nervously, still worried that someone lived there and that we were invading.

"Guys! Even if someone does live here, I think they would understand if we explained ourselves," I said, already munching loudly on a cracker.

"Oh, you mean, 'Hi, we are from the future or the past, we don't really know. We have been traveling through time trying to prevent our parents and little sister from dying?'" Kate said with sass.

"Yeah, exactly that!" I responded sarcastically. She was always trying to be *so* smart.

With a handful of crackers to go, I began to wander around the house in search of some clues of human life. I walked down a wide hallway that led to a huge bedroom. When I walked in, I was startled to see Amanda and Anne sitting quietly on the edge of the king bed. Creepy much?

I literally jumped backward a whole foot and dropped the two crackers I had left onto the carpeted floor! At first sight, I thought they might be the people that lived there. Though I had tried to convince my sisters that an explanation would work, in all honesty, I was not sure that anyone would believe our story.

"Hi!" Amanda said, excitedly rising from the bed. "This will be a great place to eat and sleep for the night!"

"How in the world did you know where we were?" I asked suspiciously.

"Well, for one, we kind of have magical powers, so we know things. Secondly, we are very familiar with the places that the Time Warp often takes people," Anne answered.

By this time, my sisters had heard me talking to someone, and ran to join me. They were also relieved that it was only Anne and Amanda.

"You mean to tell us that there have been others that have been in the same situation as us?" Christal asked.

"Oh honey, so many people lose people they love every single minute. We do the best we can to help those we are able to. It's unfortunate that the Time Warp's capacity isn't bigger," Amanda told us.

How had we not heard of anyone who had gone through this before? Don't you think it would be in the news or something? I had so many questions left unanswered.

"Well, what are you waiting for? Go eat dinner!" Anne suggested. As soon as we turned toward the kitchen, I looked back to see if Anne and Amanda were coming with us, but they were gone. It always seemed that they just gave us the least amount of information possible before they'd disappear again. But regardless of not knowing all of the facts, I was still appreciative that we'd been given the chance to save my parents and sister.

Chapter Ten

Kate

Morning came way too fast, and Anne and Amanda had still not reappeared, but we knew what we had to do. We had a nice filling dinner and a comfortable night's sleep. The house was so large that we'd each gotten our own bedroom, with a king size bed and private bathroom. Unfortunately, despite the perfectly fluffed pillows and delicate comforter, it was still hard for me to fall asleep in such a foreign place.

I kept trying to visualize that I was back home in my own bed and that everything was back to normal. Mom would be coming in in the morning to wake me up for school and my teacher would be waiting for me at the classroom door ready to give me a high-five and say hello. Of course, I knew it was not the truth, but it helped me fall asleep since counting sheep didn't work. Every time I tried to picture a sheep, I couldn't help but imagine it going through a Time Warp, and that sure was not helping me get any shut eye.

Upon waking up in what was now my new reality, we ate a delicious and fruity breakfast. I had warm peanut butter toast, a sweet, red apple, and a mix of fresh berries. I made extra sandwiches and packed more food in the bag that I put the book in, just in case we weren't able to find food for a while.

During my search for plastic bags for the food, I came across $200 in a drawer. Anne and Amanda probably left it for us. When Izzy found out, the first thing she said was, "Yay! Now we can buy clean clothes! I mean Jess must feel gross after falling into the water."

Jess just shrugged. She had been dirtier after soccer games. But I am sure none of us would mind a change of clothes and something cozier to sleep in. We hadn't thought of clothes and other necessities when we first jumped into the Time Warp at our house.

After taking warm showers, we decided to venture out into the city to find a clothing store. We walked toward the city through what felt like countless neighborhoods. A half an hour later we found ourselves surrounded by skyscrapers, stores, and restaurants. I had no doubt that this was the future, based on the incredible modern architecture and unusual greenery planted on the outer walls of several buildings. However, the smell in the city was AWFUL. The air smelled like a mix of garbage, gas fumes, and cigarette smoke. Some of the people around us were even wearing masks, which we suspected was to prevent breathing the contaminated air. What kind of future was this? It was no wonder they had planted trees and other greenery everywhere, likely to help conceal the stench and provide fresh oxygenated air.

As we walked on the sidewalks, cars with empty driver's seats passed us by. It was odd to see a car without someone at the wheel and took us by surprise. The cars did look pretty sweet though. The wheels lit up in bright colors and their sleek designs were beyond anything I had ever seen. There was even one car that was see-through with windows all around.

I was so busy taking in my surroundings that I almost missed a store painted pink, with a neon sign that said TJ's Apparel.

"Does this place look good to you guys?" Christal asked.

"Sure!" I responded, nodding along with Izzy and Jess.

The doors opened automatically as soon as we approached and a little bell rang to signal our arrival. Once inside, Izzy immediately spotted a silver, shimmery, sequined dress. She practically ran us over to get to it and held it up to her body with a smile like she had just been given a puppy.

Izzy rolled her eyes and dramatically pouted when we told her that it might not be the best outfit for time travel.

The lady working at the store was the only other person there. She glared and looked down her nose at us the whole time, like she was expecting us to run out of the store with stolen jewelry. She looked like she was probably our mom's age, but her face was pulled tight as if her skin was too small for her skull. She was plastered with makeup, had eyelashes that looked like spider legs, and was wearing multi-colored pants that I could not even begin to describe.

"Can I help you ladies find something?" she asked after we had been there a few minutes.

"Oh, we are just looking for some new clothes!" Izzy said.

"Mmhmm. Okay, well, let me know if there is anything in particular I can help you find," she offered as she stepped away to find a vantage point where she could keep a careful eye on us.

We wandered around the store and saw clothes that were like nothing we had ever seen before. There were sparkles everywhere, neon shirts, a lot of floral patterns, and other items that were definitely designed for the future. We were able to find most of our clothing style choices in an area labeled "Decades." It featured clothing from the past that had been gently used, but perfect for us, since it was actually our current style.

After about an hour of shopping, laughing at different outrageous outfits and trying clothes on, we had all picked out and changed into fresh outfits. Given that we were purchasing used clothing, it only cost us about $60 total. Call us bargain shoppers—Mom would be so proud!

We still needed heavier jackets in case we found ourselves in a cold place again. So, we went to a store a few doors down and I not only found a fuzzy thin jacket, but also purchased some gray sweatpants with a simple light blue sweatshirt. It is difficult to know what you might need when you're traveling through time, but I figured I would at least be comfortable and able to adapt to weather changes. My sisters also bought jackets and warmer garments.

As soon as we had everything we needed, we decided to return to the house so that we could create the Time Warp away from the curious eyes of other people. Plus, we needed to pick up our bag of food and the items we grabbed from the house for our travels. Christal found another backpack that we decided to fill with more food and water bottles just in case. We also stuffed both backpacks full of the new clothes we had bought.

We took our last bathroom breaks while we still had a civilized bathroom to use and Christal and I slung the backpacks that we had prepared over our shoulders.

I grabbed Izzy's hand, Izzy grabbed Christal's hand, and Christal completed the chain by holding hands with Jess. We thought about our parents, and ta-da, the Time Warp opened yet again.

This time I jumped in first, with my sisters following behind without breaking our chain of linked hands.

At some point during our travel through the Time Warp, we disconnected, and I landed alone by a sign that said, "Times Square." I was in New York City and seemed to be right in the middle of the hustle and bustle. Fortunately, my sisters were all close enough to be able to find me in the crowd and we had all somehow managed to land on our feet.

I glanced around at all the people filling the sidewalks. Everyone seemed to be speed walking, with their eyes either staring down at their phones or tracking the next person they needed to rudely rush pass. Therefore, it wasn't surprising that no one even noticed our abrupt landing. People were too busy with their own agenda to care about anyone else's.

"Let's find someone who looks like they could tell us the date and time!" Izzy said. My sisters agreed that I should try to read people's minds to make sure they were nice and safe before we approached them. We figured that was what Mom and Dad would want us to do.

Summoning my ring's powers, I read the mind of a teenage girl first; she seemed slightly older than Christal, holding her phone in front of her face and walking down the sidewalk: *I still can't believe Amy did that. Lizzy is my best friend. When I get back to school, she is in for it. I can't wait to tell the whole school what she did.*

Well... she did not seem to be in the mood to be helpful. Therefore, I attempted to read the mind of a young man walking down the street wearing headphones. It was weird reading his mind because he was just singing along to some rap lyrics in his head. I didn't think that he would even hear us if we tried to ask him for help. However, I must add, he was a pretty good rapper (at least in his own head!).

I tried one more teenager. She was slumped under the weight of a heavy backpack as she made her way down the street. She looked like she was on her way to study at a library or school. She had her hair in two long braids and was speeding through crowds like she was on a critical mission. Though I wasn't sure if she would have time to help us, she appeared to be a safe option. I quickly tried to read her mind: *I can't believe I forgot about this paper. I now have six hours to write a ten-page paper. This is going to kill my grade. I hope they have my spot open at the library.*

She seemed too stressed, so I chose yet another person: an older lady walking next to an elderly man. They both looked very rich, wearing attire meant for a night at the opera house. Each was wearing what looked like a very expensive shiny silver watch. Perfect, since we needed to know the time.

Her mind: *Ooh, ouch, ow. My knee hurts today.* I decided that she was definitely not dangerous, and it seemed that she would be helpful and kind. Well, enough anyway.

I told my sisters that she was "the one" before she walked too far down the street. Fortunately, she *was* going at a slow pace. We quickly walked over to her and the older man. Christal spoke first, in her most innocent and polite voice, "Excuse me, ma'am. My sisters and I were wondering if perhaps you would be so kind to tell us the date and time." By now, we had stopped them on the sidewalk. I could tell that people were frustrated with us, because we were blocking part of the busy sidewalk and making people circle around our huddle.

"Oh, okay, why yes, today is Monday the 15th of April," the woman shared. At this point, I could feel my heart racing. "It's, let's see, 6:05 p.m.," she continued after squinting down at her fancy watch. That was the day. The day of our parent's crash. The day that they died.

"I know this is a really weird question, but what year is it?" I asked her, trying to talk over the loud traffic and honking cabs.

She looked at me surprised, "It's 2007 dear. Are you girls okay?"

"Yes, we are fine! Thank you. Just trying to figure something out!" Christal responded. The woman gave a sideways glance at her presumed husband.

We were SO close. Unfortunately, we were still SO far. We were physically far from our home in Michigan, and it was already past the time of the crash. Even though Izzy could manipulate time, the book said nothing about reversing time, only slowing, and fast forwarding it.

We thanked the kind couple again and walked into a crowd-less alleyway. Unfortunately, the alleyway was also very eerie and creepy. It smelt like a mixture of trash and poop and it seemed drastically darker than the main street. No one had to ask me twice to get out of there.

Back into the Time Warp we went.

Chapter Eleven

Christal

My hands sank into the powdered sugar sand. It wasn't as soft as it looked, I thought, as I rubbed my tailbone after the fall.

Within seconds, I could feel the sun beaming against my pale skin. I could hear the soothing sound of the waves as they crested on the shore, rushing up the beach to tickle my fingertips. I quickly peeled off my jacket. I had a pink t-shirt on underneath with some thick black leggings, so I was already sweating. My black slip-on shoes were filling with sand with every wave; I could feel the sand wedging itself between my toes.

Wait, THIS LOOKS LIKE AN OCEAN!?! Or could it even be Lake Michigan? I licked my finger to find out. Saltier than a fry at our favorite fast-food restaurant, and conclusively, the ocean.

Where were we though? I stood up abruptly,

brushed sand from my leggings, slipped off my shoes to carry them and walked a short distance to Kate, Jess, and Izzy.

"Where do you think we are?" I asked my sisters.

"No clue. Could be any ocean near the equator, given how hot it is here," Kate answered.

"Maybe we should walk around a bit since we can't get back in the Time Warp yet anyways. There might be some sort of civilization?" I suggested. We knew this wasn't where we wanted to be, but we also knew that there wasn't a huge rush.

My sisters agreed and we began to walk the beach in a new direction, with each step leaving four sets of footprints behind us.

There was sand all around us, but far in the distance we could see what appeared to be a very large beach house.

As we peered ahead, we could see that the house was very well kept. It looked like it had four stories, with four white pillars supporting the height of the house, from the roof down to the sandy ground.

We walked closer to the mansion, which we found to be larger than our house. It looked more precious and beautiful than any house I had ever seen before. The exterior walls were a bright white and were partially covered in river rock of many colors, some bright and others dull. It sparkled like a diamond in the sunlight. Much like our skin that was now glazed with sweat.

The house looked empty, with no lights shining from the windows. It was hard to tell if anyone was living there. Then again, I can imagine when you live on a beach you probably don't spend too much time inside. I know that I wouldn't!

We went up on the front porch to the door and rang the doorbell, looking around for any signs of human life, or any life for that matter. We could hear the echo of the musical doorbell tones from where we stood outside as we pressed the silver button again.

We waited anxiously for someone to come to the door. After about two minutes we grew impatient, so we invasively peered through the tinted windows on either side of the door. Kate rang the doorbell in a third attempt before we all began knocking.

"Maybe we should just try to go to a new location," I said. I knew that this tropical location was nowhere near our home. It was not looking like this place would provide a clue or assistance in finding our parents.

"I agree. I feel like we are just wasting our time here. The Time Warp should be ready by now," Kate added.

We retreated to the beach out front, held hands, and thought of our parents.

I watched the Time Warp begin to form in its colorful amazement. When it began to swirl we were ready to jump in. I led the way and jumped into the abyss. A ping of pain hit my chest as I was thrown onto my back.

"Christal! Are you okay?" Kate immediately ran up to my limp body.

"Wh...what...just happened?" I stammered.

"I have no clue. It spit you out like Izzy spits

out mom's meatloaf," Kate could hardly contain her chuckles. "Dude, your face as you flew through the air was hilarious."

I rolled my eyes but couldn't hide a slight smile before I began to chuckle too. Kate always made me laugh with her subtle humor. Though my back was now aching, it felt good to laugh.

"Well, I am guessing the Time Warp is not an option at the moment," Izzy stated. "But why? That was so weird."

Kate grabbed the special book out of her backpack. She skimmed through the pages, quickly trying to find something that made sense of this situation. She was unsuccessful.

We went back up to the door of the house and tried knocking a few more times. Still, no one came to the door. We sat on the porch steps for probably an hour, waiting for someone to come home, continually scanning the area hoping to see someone approaching. We expected a car to drive up the long empty gravel driveway at any time, but no one ever came. This was the only house in the area, as far as we could see.

Getting hungry, we pulled out the sandwiches and snacks that we had packed and began to eat. If we were going to wait, we might as well wait with full stomachs.

We watched the sun set over the horizon as we ate and before we knew it, the pink skies were the only sign that the sun had once been out. The air was beginning to chill, and I felt shivers creep up my arms.

"Should we try to create the Time Warp again?" I asked, hesitantly.

"Um, not unless you want to go first again!" Izzy said laughing. "I'm not about to get tossed onto my back!"

"Yeah, I'm with Izzy on this one. I'd rather wait and see if Anne and Amanda show up," Jess added.

Despite still wondering if we should try again, I accepted their concerns.

I knew we were running out of options though and figured that since we were already guilty of breaking into one house in the past 24 hours, it wouldn't hurt that bad to do it again. Last time it worked out well for us, so maybe this time it would too.

I stood carefully and walked back up to the door. Before I tried opening the door, I rang the doorbell one last time. Yet again, there was no sound of life inside so I turned the doorknob, hoping with everything I had inside my heart that it would open. The knob stuck at first, but then gave way, releasing the door. I slowly proceeded to push the heavy wooden door forward while my sisters hovered right behind me.

My immediate impression was that the house looked very bare and empty. There were a few white folding chairs in the entrance room, but nothing that showed signs of anyone living there. As we ventured further into the house, we found a living room containing a comfortable looking couch and two cushy light brown chairs. The couch looked so cozy as I rushed over to rest my aching behind. I made quite a production of flopping down on the couch and lying lifelessly. Those cement porch steps had been punishing my already sore back and tailbone.

I could hear my sisters laughing in the background, until we saw two shadows appear on the back wall. Oh no! We were wrong. Someone *was* there! My heart raced and my hands trembled with fear. I sat straight up on the couch, organizing an explanation speech in my head. The two shadows moved closer, casually walking past us before they sat down on the two chairs across from me.

It was Anne and Amanda.

What a relief. We all took a deep breath and began to relax as we realized it was them. They really needed to stop sneaking up on us like this!

Amanda and Anne just stared at us blankly for a minute. It was an awkward silence for all of us. Then Amanda's face lit up with a bright smile while Anne looked annoyed; this was nothing unusual because this is how they'd behaved nearly every time we'd seen them. Finally, I couldn't stand it any longer, so I broke the silence, "Hey... what are you guys doing here?"

"Oh, we're just here to present you with your new home... momentarily of course. Uh, you see, there is a slight problem with the Time Warp...," Anne said nervously, shyly laughing as one does when they are trying to hide something. "Someone tried to take horses into the Time Warp, and it messes with the whole system. We just don't know how long it will take to find them and get them out of time travel."

We all waited in shock for them to continue explaining. It was definitely a strange predicament.

"So, you should all stay here and do whatever you wish. We will be back when the Time Warp is safe again. Don't worry, it really does not matter how long it takes you to find your parents. Time only goes by for you in the place you are at. Think of it like a little tropical vacation!" Amanda cheerfully explained.

"Speaking of where we are at... well, where are we?" Kate questioned.

"There is not an exact name for it. When the Time Warp is not working, there is no concept of time. Therefore, you are not anywhere that you would be able to recognize, as it isn't actually a real place. This island is essentially just a part of the Time Warp's magic," Anne answered.

"Well, we should get back to trying to fix the Time Warp. We will check in on you girls soon," Amanda said before they both waved and disappeared into thin air again.

Amanda told us to do whatever we wanted to do, so once the magical duo departed from our new temporary house, we did.

First, we wandered around the house, bantering over which rooms we would each sleep in. The house was so large, we were each able to have our own bedroom with a king size bed and bathroom again. Not to mention, a large walk-in closet (for all *three* of our shirts-HA!).

While all my sisters were checking out and getting settled in their bedrooms, I gazed around at mine. It had light purple paint on the walls, while the floor was a dark hardwood. It was quite charming.

In the middle of the room, there was a plush bed with a soft purple quilt that matched the color of the walls. The quilt was covered in yellow stars, and there were pillows to match. I flung myself onto my bed. It was difficult to know how long it had actually been, but it already felt like forever since we had been home. As I laid my head on the pillow, my mind wandered to thoughts of my parents. I felt like I had not even had a moment to grieve their loss, as the hope of the Time Warp had been stringing me along since we found out about their accident. What if we were never able to find them? Would we be stuck in the Time Warp forever? What if one of my sisters or I got hurt in the Time Warp? What happens then? What will we tell our parents if we are able to save them? They would never believe this, especially with their science-minded brains. Magic never would make any sense to them, as it isn't factual and concrete.

There were so many questions that could not be answered and I began to cry. I had always known what to do. I was young, but I was a natural leader. However, this was unfamiliar territory. I wanted to stay strong for my sisters, but this moment made me realize how weak I was in the face of what we were really dealing with.

Chapter Twelve

Jess

My bedroom here was so much cooler than the one I had at home. It had dark blue walls with an awesome rainbow rug covering most of the hardwood floor. There were white book shelves from floor to ceiling on the wall opposite the bed, just waiting to be filled with books and other treasures. A large walk-in closet featured a tall mirror hanging on the back wall. After spending a little time checking it all out, I headed back downstairs to the living room.

I immediately noticed four piles of clothing folded neatly side by side on the coffee table. A pile for each of us, I guessed. *Smooth.* My wardrobe was slowly growing! I snatched the sportiest looking pile and flipped through the shirts. I held them up to my nose. They smelled so fresh and clean like they were just removed from the dryer. Then, I lifted my own shirt to my nose to smell it. Ripe! It smelled like Parmesan cheese over rotten egg with a splash of vinegar on top! Must have been from sitting outside sweating earlier without deodorant.

I quickly went back to my bedroom and changed into the cozy new red t-shirt and a pair of soccer shorts that I could sleep in. I tossed the dirty clothes aside, starting a pile in the corner of my room. Just my style, I thought as I stood in front of the mirror; Anne and Amanda sure knew me well! I wished I knew them half as much, but they kept disappearing!

My eyes were beginning to get droopy, so I knew it was almost time for bed. However, I was still hungry, so a nighttime snack seemed like a good idea. I assumed all my sisters were already tucked away in their rooms since the house was eerily quiet. I think we had all needed some quiet, alone time in our rooms. After raiding the kitchen pantry, I ate a banana and peanut butter toast to satisfy my hunger for the night before going upstairs to bed.

I checked in on Christal to see if she was still awake. Her door was open, but she was not in there. I peeked into Kate's and Izzy's rooms; they were already in bed sleeping. In fact, Izzy was lying on top of the comforter, still in the clothes she had been wearing all day. I flipped her bedroom light off before heading back down the hall upstairs. The day's adventures must have wiped them out too.

I glanced at the huge grandfather clock up against the wall and noticed that it was nearly midnight. I began to worry where Christal could possibly be as I ventured back downstairs to find her.

I passed through the hall leading to the front door where I saw a note on the side table:

Izzy, Kate, and Jessica,
I went outside for a walk (in case you were wondering). I will be back soon.

Love you,
Christal

That was weird. Why would she go outside? I didn't feel comfortable going to bed without Christal safely back in the house.

I walked out the front door of the house onto the porch and looked around. It was so dark out there, and I was not a fan of the dark, especially knowing there was deep water nearby. It felt like something straight out of a scary movie. When we were at home, I couldn't even go down into the basement at night without sprinting up the stairs like I was running for my life.

Just like in most scary movies, I walked towards the dark figure sitting on the beach as soon as I saw it. But, as we all know, that does not end well for *most* characters in the scary movies.

Chapter Thirteen

Jess

"Christal?" I whispered—and hoped.

She turned her head away from the water to face me.

"Hey Jess," she responded with a small, quiet smile.

"Why are you out here so late?" I asked, as I sat down and leaned back into the cold sand next to Christal.

"Just thinking," she said, gazing up at the millions of twinkling stars in the endless black sky.

I ran my fingers gently through the sand and pondered for a few minutes before saying anything more. The calming effect of the sound of the waves lapping onto the beach partially relieved the anxiety I was feeling. Yet, in these moments of silence, I could not stop the tears from puddling in my eyes.

"Are you thinking about Mom and Dad too?" I asked.

"Yeah. I just miss them so much. I have hope that

we will see them again after all of this, but when? I miss being home with them and having them kiss me goodnight. I miss having them tell me they love me. Now, I regret all of the times that I was upset at Mom for stupid things. Or when I rolled my eyes at one of Dad's silly jokes. I took them for granted, and now they are gone."

It hurt me to see Christal being so tough on herself. She always carried so much weight as the oldest sibling.

"I feel the same way, Christal. I would give anything just to be back at home with them right now."

"I just can't help but think: why us? Why them?" Christal continued.

"I don't know—it doesn't seem fair. But try not to feel bad about taking them for granted. They know we love them."

All Christal could manage was a nod, as I watched a small tear run down the side of her freckled cheek in the light of the moon.

We sat there quietly for a few more minutes listening to the waves. "So, anyways, what are *you* doing out here so late?" Christal asked me, eventually breaking the silence.

"I just stopped by your room to say goodnight and realized you were gone. Then, I was all worried, so I had to find you. I'm glad I did."

Christal just smiled and nodded in return. I was getting cold in my shorts and my droopy eyes weren't getting any less droopy. "Well, goodnight Christal. I need to go to bed before I fall asleep right here in the sand. Be safe out here please."

"Night, Jess. See you in the morning," Christal turned back around and faced the water as I stood up and walked back to the house, wiping the sand from my legs and bottom with each step.

Chapter Fourteen

Izzy

The sun was shining brightly through my window as I slowly peeled my eyes open. I looked at a digital clock that was glaring at me from the night-stand next to the bed; it was 10:04. Wow, I slept in late! Usually, 8:30 was considered "sleeping in" for me when it wasn't a school day. I hadn't even remembered falling asleep!

After also realizing I had slept in my clothes, I changed into one of the outfits that Anne and Amanda had left in my personal wardrobe pile. Jean shorts and a pink t-shirt were perfect for what I hoped would be a beach day. There was even a bathing suit in my pile that I could come back and grab later.

I briskly bounded down the stairs to go to the kitchen, worried I might have missed breakfast. There was Christal, standing by the stove cooking eggs. I could smell bread toasting in the toaster too. My mouth salivated at the thought of adding a smear of butter and watching it melt on the warm toast.

"Good morning!" she greeted me.

"Good morning," I replied creakily, still waking up my voice.

"Have a seat!" Christal gestured to one of the seats at the round kitchen table. "Breakfast will be ready in a few minutes."

"Smells yummy, thank you. Where are Kate and Jess? I noticed they weren't in their rooms."

"Oh, they went for a walk along the beach to explore. They should be back any minute. They tried waking you up, but we all know you're a deep sleeper," Christal giggled.

I could not even deny that. There was a time, when I was six years old, that I slept through almost my entire birthday party. I was awake when the first person arrived, fell asleep on the couch, and woke up just in time for cake and ice cream. Everyone said they had tried waking me up, and even felt for my pulse to make sure I was still alive. I was, of course, bummed that I had missed most of my party. But at least I woke up in time for cake, ice cream, and presents. So, what six-year-old would really complain?

I sat down at the nicely set table which included a vase full of light pink and purple hibiscus flowers. "Where did you find the flowers?" I asked.

"I also went exploring this morning, before anyone was awake. By the way, the sunrise is beautiful here," Christal explained.

"Geez, you must have gotten up so early! What time did you even go to bed?"

"Uh, one or two. I kind of forgot to even look," Christal said, and I jokingly shook my head and rolled my eyes.

"Why did you not sleep in?!" I exclaimed.

"I couldn't really sleep well. Kept waking up. Finally decided to just get up and start my day. I hate sleeping away from home."

I understood what she meant, but conversely had no issues falling asleep—literally anywhere.

Just then, Kate and Jess walked through the front door. "It is *so* pretty here! We saw so many birds and frogs and different animals!" Jess skipped down the hallway to the table. Christal put two eggs and a piece of toast on every plate, and we all settled down to eat.

"So, what are we going to do today?" I asked as I added that eagerly anticipated smear of butter to my toast.

"Um, I guess whatever we want to do. I think maybe go to the beach or something and swim. We're stuck here, so we might as well enjoy it, right?" Christal suggested.

We all nodded, with mouths full of much appreciated warm home cooked food. For being only a sixth grader, Christal sure could cook!

* * *

I went back up to my room to slip on that bathing

suit under my shorts and t-shirt, grabbed a beach towel I found in a dresser drawer, and ran down to the beach where my other sisters were already relaxing in the sun.

The sand enveloped my feet as I leaped across the beach to join my sisters. It already felt like lava, and it wasn't even midday yet.

"Nice of you to finally join us," Christal commented sarcastically.

"Yes, I know you appreciate me finally gracing you with my presence," I said while doing a curtsy. I spread out my towel across the burning sand next to Kate and quickly laid down to prevent the loss of skin on the bottom of my feet. Before I could even fully lay down, Christal tossed a plastic bottle at me. Sunscreen. Of course, Christal would remember to bring that and insist we put it on. Her maturity both impressed and annoyed me.

I caught it in mid-air and stuck my tongue out at her smiling face, before beginning to reluctantly apply it to my pale body. I knew I needed to put it on for my own well-being, but I hated it because it made me feel so sticky! I knew the sand would stick to me now like flies on poop!

It didn't take long in the scorching sun before I practically flew into the icy cold water. I went in up to my waist and then decided to see how much deeper I could go.

I took one step too many. My foot slipped over an edge and down I went, sinking in well over my head. I tried to grab the shallow edge to push myself back towards the surface and struggled to kick up, seemingly making no progress. The current felt like it was pushing me further and further down and away. It felt like I was drowning, and I couldn't get up onto the shallow ledge no matter how hard I kicked and paddled. My eyes, which I had opened to try and see my way up, were absolutely burning as if someone had sprayed pepper spray directly into them. I could barely keep them open more than a small slit.

Suddenly, I heard murmurs of splashing and voices that weren't coming from me. Christal, Jess, and Kate found my hands and somehow pulled me up. I gasped to catch my breath as soon as I was above the water.

"Thank you, thank you," I cried between raspy breaths and tears once they got me to the beach and laid me down on my towel. My whole body was shaking, more from fear than cold I think.

I did not want to go back into that water. Ever.

My sisters looked equally traumatized, all breathing hard from their efforts and panic. I was just grateful they had noticed my struggle.

"Izzy, how did you get so far out?" Kate asked, once we had all caught our breath.

"I don't know. I guess I didn't realize how deep it was, until all of a sudden there was a drop off," I responded.

"Please be careful Izzy. That was so scary," Jess commented.

"I know. I don't plan to go back into the water, trust me." I certainly learned my lesson. I also felt even more grateful for my sisters than ever. They were so brave and selfless. Not only that, but I suddenly appreciated those expensive swimming lessons Mom made us do when we were younger. They may not have paid off for me, but they sure did for my sisters.

After a long day at the beach, we made our way back to the house, exhausted and hungry after accidentally missing lunch. It was nearing 5 o'clock, so Christal and Kate started making dinner, while Jess and I set the table. Time always flies on the beach.

I went to change out of my bathing suit and into something more comfortable before dinner, as did my sisters.

Once dinner was ready, we ate slowly, dragging our spaghetti covered forks from our plates to our mouths. It was a much needed warm and comforting meal for us, as it was a simple dish that our parents would make at least once a week—which is why my sisters knew how to make it. We didn't talk a whole lot during dinner; our day on the hot beach was exhausting. Even though we mostly just laid around, sun combined with my scary near-drowning incident just made us all so worn-out.

It was only 6:30 when we finished dinner, but I could have gone to bed right then and there. My face and shoulders were starting to blush light red, and my back and neck had red Dalmatian spots where I could tell I'd missed when spreading my greasy sunscreen. I certainly wasn't pale anymore! However, I am not sure if red is a better look on me.

There was still some daylight after dinner, and it was too early to *actually* go to bed, so we decided to take a walk together. The island was so big, and there was so much more to explore. We walked along the beach for a while, tip-toeing our feet in the waves as they crashed into the shore. Stars and the moon began to emerge in the pale blue sky, glimmering through a few clouds here and there. The sound of various bird calls, along with the rushing of the waves, combined for a sound that seemed like it was coming from a sleep sound-machine. If we had to be stuck somewhere, this really wasn't the worst place to be.

The stars came out in full beauty as the night sky continued to creep in above us. We took a break on a small hill to gaze at the sky. We had a view of "our" house on one side and part of the shoreline that we had yet to visit on the other.

"Do you see the light coming from over there?" Kate questioned, pointing to the spot she was referring to.

I glanced over to where she was directing us and noticed a small bit of orange light and a wisp of smoke rising above it towards the moon.

"That has to be a fire!" Christal said with excitement. "Maybe someone else is here!"

I had not thought about it before, but if the Time Warp really was not working, other people may be stopped in their tracks too. I remembered how Anne and Amanda had said we weren't the only ones journeying to find our loved ones. However, it seemed strange that they didn't mention that we were sharing the island with others.

"Do you think we should see who it is?" I asked. We all looked around at each other for a moment in hesitation.

"Maybe...we should wait for daylight," Kate suggested. "Just to be safe."

I could not disagree with Kate's logic, but was also a tad disappointed that I would have to wait until tomorrow to find out who was on the island with us.

Chapter Fifteen

Kate

I could smell the indisputable aroma of sizzling bacon and eggs from my bedroom. I changed out of my pajamas and sped downstairs to the kitchen where Christal was cooking again. What would we do without her and her love of cooking?

It was only about seven in the morning, but we were all anxious to find other people on the island. I don't consider myself to be especially social, but I was looking forward to talking to people other than my sisters—no offense to them.

We finished eating breakfast, cleaned up, and prepared a few items for our venture out into the unknown. I packed a small black backpack with some water and snack bars, just in case we were gone longer than expected.

I led up the same hill that we had been sitting on the night before so we could get a good view of where we were headed. Now that it was light out, we no longer had the fire to guide us. However, I was still able to spot a small bit of smoke rising through the trees from where a fire was dwindling.

We walked toward the smoke, little by little, taking breaks as needed. It really was not that far to walk, but there were many small hills which posed more of a challenge. Jess, of course, with her soccer trained legs, was powering through regardless, and making it look easy as pie.

As we got closer, we could see a house very similar to the one that we were staying in. There were a few people passing a soccer ball on the beach in front of the house.

As we approached, they waved and smiled at us. One of the boys kept the soccer ball at his feet.

"Hey! You guys must be new here!" one boy who looked my age said. "I'm Tommy," he greeted us with a slightly awkward nod now that we were within ten feet of one another.

"Hi Tommy. I'm Christal. These are my sisters Kate, Jess, and Izzy," my sister said, gesturing toward each one of us as she introduced us.

"Cool. Wanna play with Alex, Mitch, Brady, and me? We were about to start a game."

"I will!" Jess immediately answered. I was not a huge fan of soccer, so I was going to sit this one out. Plus, I wanted to figure out why they said we were "new." Didn't the Time Warp breakdown for all of us at the same time?

The boys and Jess all began to play, with a few other boys and girls joining them as the game began.

I sat down in the sand with Jess and Christal in a spot where we could view the soccer game. They had set up a field on the beach using cones they must have gotten from Anne and Amanda. The players were already sweating from running around, and it wasn't even that hot out yet. Before long, the sand would be too scorching to play on—it would probably feel like a hot bed of coals on their bare feet.

"Hey. Who are you?" A girl, with long blond hair down to her hips and bright blue eyes standing out against her slightly freckled face, approached the three of us. She stood over us with arms folded, scanning us from head to toe.

"Uh, hi, I am Kate, this is Christal, and this is Izzy. Our other sister is playing soccer right now. We are living in a house on the other side of the island."

"Oh. Well, why are you here?"

Christal chirped in next, "We're trying to save our parents. The Time Warp broke. Aren't you here for the same reason?" Christal raised her eyebrows at the girl who was coming off as very standoffish.

"Yeah, I guess. But we've been here for a while," the girl responded, glancing over towards the soccer players.

"Why? What do you mean a while?" Christal inquired.

"I don't know. We came here maybe like, a year ago? The Time Warp had broken down, and we really liked it here and all the people we'd met. We figured it didn't hurt to stay for a bit. I guess it has just been a little longer than we thought we would stay."

I was confused. Why would they stay here when they had someone to save? It didn't make sense. I was surprised that Anne and Amanda would even allow that.

"Who are you with?" Izzy asked.

"My brother Mitch and my sister Lizzy. I'm Julie by the way." Julie was slowly loosening up and becoming a little bit more friendly. Though she still had a slight sassy tone. I could definitely tell that Julie was the oldest of her siblings. She looked like she was a few years older than all of us. Mitch looked more like my age, and we had yet to meet Lizzy.

"Who are all these other people?" Izzy questioned, referring to the ten or so other people on the beach.

"They've been here a while too," Julie responded. "We all live in this house and the house behind it. Unlike *some* people, we didn't get our own private residence, which I am assuming you did," Julie rolled her eyes. I supposed the friendliness was over.

"I've gotta go check on Lizzy. See you guys later," Julie said as she turned and walked back towards their temporary house.

Chapter Sixteen

Kate

I still could not understand how people could stay on the island knowing that their loved ones were gone. I could not go a minute without thinking about my parents and little sister, and as much as this island was cool and all, I wanted my parents and Lucy back more than anything else.

Jess returned to where we were sitting—her sweaty face looked like a freshly glazed doughnut. "You *have* to meet these people. They are *so* nice!" Izzy exclaimed in between heavy breaths. "Tommy said we could come to their place for lunch if we want! I told him I would talk to you guys first."

"Sure, let's go!" Izzy said excitedly. I knew immediately what she was thinking: BOYS.

We quickly strolled over to meet the boys where they had been playing soccer. Izzy led the way. Tommy was there, along with a few other guys who looked about the same age.

Tommy introduced us to Mitch (Julie's brother), Alex, Brady, Jacob, and Cam. We soon found out that Alex and Brady were twin brothers. We also found out that Jacob and Cam were the older brothers of two much younger sisters, Lilly and Cassie. Tommy was completely on his own. I don't know what I would've done if I didn't have my sisters with me.

Once the introductions were finished, we headed into their beach house for some lunch. The boys and their sisters had similar food in their house as we had in ours. We all passed around sandwich ingredients and chips until our plates were covered in carbs and meat.

"So, what happened to your parents?" I overheard Cam ask Christal from where they sat on the couch side by side. We had all settled at either the kitchen table or the living room couches to eat our sandwiches.

"We came home from school to an answering machine message from them and it sounded like they were in a car accident. We weren't sure if they had passed away until we met Anne and Amanda. They told us all about the Time Warp, so we left pretty soon after that," Christal answered with watering eyes.

"I'm sorry, Christal. That stinks," Cam truly did look empathetic.

"I just hope we are able to save them," she continued. There were a few moments of silence while they both took a bite of their sandwiches. "Why are you and your siblings here?" Christal asked once she finished chewing. I was just glad to see she didn't talk with her mouth full—she was still working on that, much to Mom's dismay.

"Our parents were on vacation overseas for their anniversary. We were at home with our Grandma when we found out that our parents had gotten really sick from something, and the doctors didn't know how to help them," said Cam. "According to the phone call she received from the authorities there, it had been too late by the time they were able to get to a hospital."

"Wow, that's awful. What did your Grandma do?"

"She's probably wondering where in the world we went!" Cam chuckled, lightening the mood a bit. "But nah, she had told us the news, and gave us some time to grieve as siblings after we all pretty much ran to Jacob's room crying. She was super sad too, obviously. Then Anne and Amanda showed up in my brother's bedroom. We left in the Time Warp from there."

"I wonder if anyone even realizes that we are missing. Like, I am so confused about how this whole thing works when we're not there. I guess that's the magic of it all," Christal pondered aloud.

"Yeah, I know right? We've tried asking Anne and Amanda about it, but it never makes 100% sense," Cam agreed.

"I feel like they always disappear before I can even ask them anything! How long have you and your siblings been here?" Christal asked.

"I'm honestly not even sure. I stopped counting days a while ago. Probably at least half a year?" Cam's answer surprised me. I couldn't believe they had been here this long. Why didn't they want to go save their parents? Christal had to have been wondering the same thing.

I decided I should stop eavesdropping on a conversation I wasn't involved in and walked over to where Izzy was sitting.

She was sitting by Lilly and Cassie, who were five and six years old. I wondered how they must feel and how much they truly understood about all of this. Probably not a whole lot. I barely understood it and I am double their age.

"Hey, I'm Kate!" I introduced myself to the girls.

"Hi!" they said excitedly. I am sure they were glad to have some older girls around. After all, they were currently being taken care of by their brothers, and who knows how that was going!

"Wanna play with us?" Lilly asked me as I sat down next to her. She held out a doll with long black mop hair and a squishy, plush body.

"Sure, I can play with you," I said. Looking at her hopeful expression, I didn't have the heart to say no. Izzy already had a doll in her hand and was following along with the little girls' imaginations. They were currently in the middle of a scene where the mom doll was telling the little girl doll to go into time-out for being mean.

Another child came over and sat by Cassie. She

looked to be around five or six years old as well. "Hi, what's your name?" Izzy asked.

"I'm Lizzy," she said, currently preoccupied by the doll she grabbed onto. I realized she must be the little sister that Julie had mentioned before. She also had long blond hair and those ocean blue eyes that apparently ran in the family.

I finally noticed Jess around the corner sitting at the kitchen table. She was talking to Tommy, Alex, and Brady while they continued to munch on salty potato chips.

I sat my doll down and decided that I was ready to go back to our house. I liked meeting new people, and was glad we came to meet them, but I wasn't a socializer like my sisters. Reading a book on the beach sounded like a much better idea. The characters in my book were the only friends I needed at the moment.

I checked in with Christal to let her know that I was headed back. She was still deep in a conversation with Cam about something. I could tell by her blushed cheeks that she already had a crush on the guy. Before I left, since I was kind of bored, I decided to listen in on her thoughts with the powers that my ring carried.

He is so cute. I can't believe he is talking to me. I hope he asks me to hang out again while we are on this island. His brown eyes are so big and handsome.

Christal's obnoxious thoughts only confirmed my assumptions.

Having finally left their house, I slowly climbed up and down the sand hills back to our temporary residence. I went up to my designated room and dug through the bookshelf to find a book I would be interested in. I ended up finding a mystery novel for teens. It looked good enough for the time being.

I headed to the beach, laid out a towel, and threw a book in front of my face for the remainder of the afternoon.

Chapter Seventeen

Izzy

I couldn't help but feel a little jealous. Christal was getting all of the attention, as always. What if I thought Cam was cute? What if I wanted to talk to him too?

Instead, I was stuck here playing dolls with the little girls. Not that I minded much, but I could have found better ways to spend my time.

I saw the way he was smiling at her and laughing when she said anything remotely funny. Typical.

As I was staring at Cam and Christal, Julie walked over and sat down on the floor next to her little sister.

"Yeah, good luck with that." She rolled her eyes after she saw me staring at the two of them.

I looked at her, pretending to be confused.

"He's the cutest one here. I know. I have been here for *way* longer than you. But all he likes to do is play soccer with his guy friends. Not interested in much else. It won't last," she explained.

"Oh, yeah," I agreed, playing along.

"Besides, he is too old for her. He is more like my age, 14 or 15 or something like that," Julie continued.

"Christal is close to that. She is the oldest of all of us," I argued now.

"Well, whatever. Good luck is all I have to say. Come on Lizzy, time to go back to the beach. I want to go swimming."

With that, she took Lizzy by the hand and headed out the door with her, much nicer, little sister. Lizzy left her doll stranded on the floor next to me, so I sat mine down as well.

Going back to the beach didn't sound like a bad idea, but I certainly wasn't going with *her*.

I passed by Kate on my way back to our house. She was sleeping with a book next to her head. She was going to be so sunburnt! I decided I would grab some sunscreen to bring out to her.

As I stepped into the front room of the house, I saw a shadow in the kitchen. I immediately jumped, as I knew where all of my sisters were currently located, and it wasn't there.

"Hi Izzy!" It was Amanda. Anne was sitting in a chair at the table. Amanda had been looking in the fridge but closed it when she saw me. "I was just checking to make sure you girls still had enough food."

"Hi, yeah, we are okay for right now. Thank you," I responded.

"So, we are able to tell you a time estimate now that we sort of know what is going on with the Time Warp. It looks like it will only be down for one more week, and then you can be safely back on your way to saving your parents," Anne said. "Could you let your sisters know?"

"Yeah, of course. Will you be back to tell us when it is safe to make the Time Warp again?"

"For sure. We will stop by a few times to make sure everything is going okay before then too. We feel so bad about this, so we want to make sure that you are all comfortable," Anne explained.

"Yeah, things have been going well! I do have a weird question for you though."

"What's up?" Amanda asked.

"Why have Julie, Mitch, and Lizzy been here for so long? Like, why have they not been trying to save their family?" I asked.

"Well, it is a little more complicated than your situation. You see, they did not have the best relationship with their parents. When their parents passed away, it was not really anything new to them. Their parents had checked out a while before that. Julie has had to pretty much raise her younger siblings on her own. That doesn't mean they don't love their parents dearly and want them back. I just don't think that Julie is ready for that reality again," Amanda answered, less peppy than normal.

"Oh, well that makes sense," I responded. Now I

almost couldn't blame her for being so sassy all the time. "What about Cam and his family?"

"Same type of situation, unfortunately. Their parents were always traveling so it was their grandmother that pretty much raised them. Whenever the Time Warp breaks down, or kids are staying a while in a certain location, we try not to push them to leave until they feel they are ready," Anne answered this time.

"Well, we must get back to work fixing the Time Warp, but thanks for passing on the message," Amanda said before they vanished into thin air yet again.

Chapter Eighteen

Christal

We had been on the island for a few days now, and I hung out with Cam most of that time. Part of me felt bad leaving my sisters so much, but I also knew that I had less than a week with Cam before we would be going our separate ways.

Cam told me that their household was going to have a bonfire at seven, and he hoped my sisters and I would join.

When I told my sisters about it, they were just as excited as I was. Aside from Jess playing soccer with the guys a few times, my sisters had stuck closer to the house the last day or so and wanted to get out and see the others again.

After dinner we walked over to their house. We could already see smoke rising from a fire pit, though it wasn't quite dark enough to see the orange flickering flames clearly yet.

"Hey Christal," Cam greeted me with a warm hug. "Hi everyone!" He waved to the rest of my sisters.

"Help yourself to some s'mores. There are some sticks over by Alex and the marshmallows and stuff are right inside the house."

"Thanks Cam!" I responded, more excited to see him than about eating s'mores—which is shocking with my obsessive love for sweets!

Although the fire wasn't roaring just yet, we sat down around the pit in some plastic lawn chairs that the guys had set up. Alex, Brady, and Jacob were already sitting around the fire, holding sticks with puffy burnt marshmallows hanging by a thread over the flames. We relaxed by the fire, as the sun continued to set, talking about our lives and where we were from. It was so interesting to learn about where the others normally lived, as well as where the Time Warp had taken them. We had our fair share of adventures, but the others definitely did too.

Alex told us about the last place that he and Brady were. They had been dropped in the middle of a seemingly endless mountain range. The boys were starving so they tried to find something to eat instead of hopping back into the Time Warp right away. They climbed down the mountain that they were on, hoping that if they went down further, they might find some sort of civilization. Nope. No luck there. Alex eventually took a tumble down the mountain, and it was then that they decided that they would find food at their next location. They did say they saw some nice views though.

Jacob, Cam, and their little sisters had been through a lot too. They had been dropped in the middle of a neighborhood that looked very unusual. All the houses were huge, looked identical, and had one large tree out front with artificial grass on the ground. Otherwise, there had not been any other plants in the neighborhood, as if they didn't exist anymore. It was a beautiful sunny day when they were there, so it was strange that not a single child or person was outside. A few cars pulled into their driveways and garages. The people got out, plugged their cars into some electric cord, and went straight into their houses. It was utterly strange.

Cam and Jacob continued to explain what they saw there. Everyone was leaning toward them across the fire, anxious to hear more about this place.

"We went up to one of the houses to see where we were, hoping that the people would be nice. This very large man opened the door with a headset attached to his bald oval head and all he said was, 'That was quick. You have my food?'" Cam said.

"Clearly, we did not have any food with us, so that was not why we were on his front doorstep. I mean, why would there be four of us if that were the case? So, we asked the dude where we were and what year it was," Jacob continued the story. "He told us hesitantly that it was 2081 and we were in Michigan."

"You could tell he was kind of annoyed at us,

especially since we weren't delivering his food from whatever app he ordered it from. When we peeked around him, we could see a kid our age sitting on a couch playing a video game that looked SO real on their huge TV," Cam explained.

"Guys, it was so weird. I hope that is not our future, because it was not good. Barely any plants, super-hot, everyone inside their houses. The air even had this weird smell, like we were in the middle of a city, but it was Michigan," Jacob continued.

Jacob and Cam continued to describe their experience. Before they left the future, they went to a restaurant with some money that Anne and Amanda had given them. They said that there were no waitresses or real people working there. Everything was robotic and they had to order their meals on a touch screen. Even the cooks were robots! The only humans in the place were a few other customers with their kids, who were completely absorbed in whatever it was they were holding—presumably the latest and greatest technology.

"Do all of you guys also have rings with powers?" Kate asked after they had finished their story.

"Yeah, but they are different than yours," Cam held out his hand for everyone to see. The ring was a simple silver band around his ring finger. I couldn't see any swirls from where I was sitting. It seemed like girls and boys were given different styles of rings.

"What are your powers?" Izzy asked. "Hopefully better than mine!"

Izzy's comment caused a ripple of giggles to pass through the group. "I can make claws out of my hands and fingers. Seems like a weird power to have, but it's actually been pretty helpful in areas we had to get away from something," Cam said.

"We could have used that a few times!" I laughed, thinking about our incident with the jaguar.

"I have the power to float a few inches above ground. It's been pretty cool," Jacob shared.

We all went through and shared what our powers were and it was neat to see that they were all pretty unique. The only two people that had the same power were Kate and, come to find out, Julie. After finding that out, I realized why Julie had been even more standoffish. She probably read our minds when we were thinking that she was sassy and rude.

After sharing a few more stories about places we had all traveled to, Cam asked if I wanted to help him grab some more marshmallows from inside the house. I eagerly accepted and we walked up to their house together. When we were just far enough away from the others, Cam grabbed my hand and squeezed it just slightly. The butterflies in my stomach took off towards the night stars and I couldn't help but blush.

Once we got to the house, we needed our hands to carry marshmallows, crackers and chocolate, so we didn't get to hold hands anymore. That was probably for the best because I really didn't want my sisters to see. Especially since Izzy had already been acting so weird towards me lately.

The night ended soon after our last round of s'mores were cooked and devoured. We were all full and struggling to keep our eyes open, so my sisters and I said goodnight and walked back to our momentary home. It had been a good, good night.

Chapter Nineteen

Christal

I woke up to Anne and Amanda sitting on the edge of my bed.

"Woah!" I popped right up, catching my breath, not expecting anyone to be in my room AT ALL.

"Ahh, sorry! I told you we should wait in the kitchen," Anne said sassily to Amanda, throwing her hands in the air.

"My bad. Sorry Christal. Didn't mean to scare you. Anyways, we have great news!" Amanda exclaimed as my heart beat started to slow back down to normal.

"The Time Warp is officially working again! You and your sisters can leave whenever you want to now!" Amanda continued.

I felt awful that my immediate reaction was a feeling of disappointment. I wasn't ready to leave the island. In all honesty, I just wasn't ready to leave Cam yet. I was beginning to see why the others had stayed so long.

It must have shown on my face because Anne asked if everything was okay and why I didn't seem happy. I didn't want to have to explain, so I told her I was just shocked it was fixed so quickly and tried to fake a smile.

"I will tell my sisters," I said. "Do you want me to tell everyone else too?"

"No, it's okay, we will make our rounds today. You will have to get ready to leave, so we will let you get right to it!" Anne said.

The girls then vanished into thin air, so I quickly changed out of my cozy pajamas, into some equally comfortable soccer shorts and a t-shirt before going to find my sisters.

Only Kate was downstairs, so I was able to tell her right away. She was relieved and ready to go. At least someone was.

Jess and Izzy woke up slightly later and when I told them the news, they wanted to leave within the next hour so we could get back to our mission.

We all started to pack our backpacks and put on some layers of clothing that we would want to have with us in preparation for any weather or situation. We were learning quickly why our parents always said that it is better to be prepared.

After we finished packing, I told the girls that I wanted to say goodbye to a few friends on the island. The girls came along, and we said our goodbyes to the friendly, and not so friendly, people we had encountered on the island. I saw Cam standing by the shore, kicking at the waves, and walked over to him.

"Hey," I said shyly, and he turned around to face me.

"Hey, Christal. I heard you are leaving," he said.

"Yeah, the Time Warp is working again; aren't you leaving too?" I asked.

"We will, just not yet. Maybe tomorrow or something," Cam pondered aloud. I questioned if that was even true.

There were a few moments of silence while we both just stared out at the seemingly endless mass of water.

"I am going to miss you, Christal. I wish we had met in our real lives," Cam said.

"I will miss you too Cam; I wish I didn't have to leave so soon," I said, leaning in for a hug. He held me tight as we hugged, and a small tear dropped from my eye. Was I really this dramatic? He was, after all, my first crush. So yes, I sure was.

Cam grabbed my hand one more time. "I hope we meet again."

"Me too," I smiled a small smile and walked away, back to my sisters.

Chapter Twenty

Jess

It felt a little strange to be getting ready to get into the Time Warp again. I couldn't help feeling nervous that it still wouldn't work, and we would end up in a black hole or something. We had been living on the island for about a week, and though that was not a long time, it was the longest we had been in any single place since we left home.

I missed my parents. I missed my bed. I missed my friends at school. I wanted to be back at home.

We went to the front of the house and held hands, with our rings secure on our fingers. We all thought of our love for our parents and the Time Warp emerged before our eyes. It was even more beautiful than I had remembered it.

"Let's go," Christal said, leading the jump.

* * *

We landed in a place so familiar this time. We were right in front of the grocery store in our hometown. Perfectly placed on the grass next to the road, we were gladly avoiding the cars passing in the street.

I looked around at my sisters, and we all shared the same shocked expression. We didn't know what time or day it was, but we were back where it had happened. This was where our parents were headed the day of the accident.

Chapter Twenty-One

Izzy

"We have to find out what day it is," Kate said almost immediately after landing. "Come on, let's go into the store."

We urgently ran across the grocery store parking lot, making sure to avoid cars pulling in and out like race cars, and quickly raced through the sliding door entrance.

"Hi, what day is it?" Kate asked the greeter at the front of the store before she could even open her mouth to welcome us.

"Hi honey, it is Monday. I lose track all the time too!" she replied with a laugh.

"No, we mean what date is it?" I asked.

She replied, "Oh, it is September 22nd," and gave us a friendly grin.

"What year is it? What time is it?" I pestered right away.

"Oh, well, hmm, it is 5:46 and the year is 2018." The woman looked very confused now.

"Thank you!" we all said in unison, and we ran back through the front doors of the grocery store.

"Guys, that is the day we lost our parents," Kate said as soon as we reached the sidewalk in front of the store.

"I think we are too late though," Christal said somberly.

"I wish my powers would let me go back in time. I can only slow time and fast forward a little. How pointless," I said in defeat, and slumped down on a bench right outside the grocery store.

"It's okay Izzy. We will just keep trying." Christal sat down next to me and put her arm around my shoulder. My other sisters squeezed onto the bench too, all beginning to tear up.

After a few minutes of sulking, we walked back towards the main street where we had landed. It was then that we noticed small pieces of headlight and scattered glass on the street that hadn't been completely cleaned up.

It was time to leave and travel to our next mystery destination.

We were so close. But not close enough.

Chapter Twenty-Two

Kate

If you have ever felt out of place somewhere, I want you to imagine our situation to be ten times worse. I've had those times when I show up somewhere, dressed way more casually than every other person in the room. It always feels so awkward.

This was *much* worse.

We were surrounded by women and little girls strolling around us wearing long plain colored dresses that looked faded from their original colors, as if they had been worn and washed a few too many times. I thought to myself...*maybe Mom was right about needing to separate colors in the washer after all.* Most of the women were also wearing elaborate hats with feathers, making them seem about ten feet taller than they really were.

The men and boys were wearing suits and caps like

they were all going to church or somewhere equally formal.

Then, there was us. Wearing jeans, t-shirts with sparkly logos, and sandy tennis shoes.

I paid enough attention in history class to know that we were certainly not in the right year, let alone century. It had to be some time in the 1800s, but it was hard to be sure, and I was not planning on asking this time around.

We stood up and brushed off our pants, having landed in the dirt, and began to walk around to check out the place. We were getting a lot of curious stares and mean glares. People pointed at us from across the dirt road.

"Outta the way!" a man yelled from high atop his carriage seat. That drew our attention to his team of horses that were headed straight towards us on the path. We quickly bolted to the side to get out of their way.

We tried to stay off the main street after that. Not only because it smelled like horse poop, but we also figured it would be best to go unnoticed as much as possible to avoid questioning.

Too late for that, I guess. A few little girls ran up behind us. "Who are you?" they asked, staring at us with curious blue eyes. The girls were wearing matching purple dresses, both flowing down to their ankles. Their light blond hair was back in a tight bun, and they looked like twins, if not at least sisters. I figured they were about five or six years old.

My sisters and I all just looked at one another like we were fish out of water. None of us really knew what was appropriate to say in this situation.

"Hi, I'm Izzy!"

"Good afternoon. I am Loyce and this is Dorothy. Why are you wearing those odd clothes?" Leave it to children to ask the blunt questions.

"Um, well..." Izzy pondered aloud. "We found these clothes somewhere."

"Oh," the girls responded in unison, looking quite confused.

"Where do you live? I have never seen you here before," one of the young girls continued pestering.

"We live... kind of far away from here. We are just visiting," I responded. "I am sorry girls, but we have to go. It was nice meeting you."

We quickly shuffled away, as if we truly had somewhere urgent to go. The girls were very sweet, but we did not want to create any problems before we could find our way out of this place.

Needing to burn a little more time, we walked around the outskirts of the main street. Peering through the gaps in buildings, we could see the bustling streets full of people of all ages. The buildings were taller than I had imagined, with large awnings hanging over the tops of stores and cafes. Even from where we were walking, I could hear the pitter-patter of the horses' hooves against the cobblestone path.

I had always been so curious about this time-period. Having read so many historical fiction and non-fiction books about the 1800 and 1900s, it was crazy to see it all in person. I'd only ever seen it in black and white movies or visualized words from a page, and now, I was staring at everything in full color.

Though I would have loved to stay and study the era, we walked a little bit further out of town and decided it was the best place to get the Time Warp going again. We silently hoped this would be the last time.

Chapter Twenty-Three

Christal

I looked around as I shot out of the Time Warp. I immediately wanted to burst into tears. I was at home again. My sisters landed close to me in the living room. The sun was shining through the kitchen window near us. I looked at the clock sitting next to our television. It was 2:10 p.m., so school hadn't let out yet. My hopes were so high. This could be it; we just needed to find out if this was the right day.

"Izzy, turn on the TV. Let's see if we can figure out what day it is," I quickly requested, as Izzy was closest to the remote.

I could tell that my sisters were also more anxious than a high schooler taking his driver's test, as the moment we had seemingly waited so long for was at the tip of our fingers.

The television screen came to color and Izzy flipped quickly through the channels looking for a channel that might show the date. After landing upon a news channel, we held our breaths as we watched the ticker at the bottom of the screen until we finally saw the date. No way! Could it be?

This was the day that it happened! And this was right around the time that our parents left that message on the answering machine. I almost couldn't believe it. Was it too good to be true?

We immediately began jumping up and down and hugging each other. At this point we all had tears rolling down our faces. We had done it. We were *so* close to getting the rest of our family back.

Within what felt like minutes, the phone began to ring. I sprinted to the phone and picked it up before the second ring. Without even saying hello, I yelled, "Mom! Dad! Be careful and watch out for any cars that might be out of control!" remembering how short her message had been before the crash.

I could hear hesitation on the other end. "Honey, be careful! Oh my, look out!"

Suddenly, there was nothing but silence on her end of the phone. I heard a click signaling the end of the call.

"Guys...I don't think it was enough time to save them. I couldn't save them," I choked out, unable to hold back tears. "We should have called them as soon as we got here."

"It's okay Christal. It's not your fault. We will just keep trying!" Kate said encouragingly, hugging me tight. My other sisters solemnly nodded in agreement.

Then the phone began to ring again. It was still sitting in the palm of my hand. I clicked the button to answer. "Hello?"

"Hi sweetheart. I am so sorry I had to hang up on you so quickly. We almost got hit by a crazy driver running a red light! Can you believe that? Some people need to be more careful. It looked like she was texting on her phone. Luckily, your Dad swerved out of the way just in time. So strange that you had just told us to be careful!"

"Mom!!!! You and Dad are okay?! Lucy is safe?" I smiled ear to ear. My sisters saw and immediately jumped up and down synchronously. Tears, the happy kind this time, began running down my cheeks.

"Yes, we are all fine. We just picked Lucy up and are on our way to the store. Wait, but what are you even doing home already, young lady?" Mom asked.

"It is a very long story. Can I tell you when you get home?" I said, not quite ready to explain it all over the phone and not wanting to distract them while they were driving.

"Sure. Wait, are those your sisters' voices I hear in the background? You are all home?"

"Yeah, we are all here."

"Well, in that case we will come straight home for an explanation before going grocery shopping," Mom said with Dad, listening in on speaker phone, adding his agreement. "On our way. Be home soon. Love you!"

"Love you too Mom!"

* * *

"Now what do we do?" Izzy asked.

"We wait for them to come home and beg them to never leave again," I answered, wiping the tears from my cheeks.

We waited there silently in the living room for what felt like forever.

We immediately perked up when we heard the front door handle begin to rattle back and forth as a key turned within it. Mom and Dad walked through the front door with our baby sister in her carrier.

"Mom! Dad!" We all bombarded them with hugs. They accepted them with confusion, giving each other the look of, 'What is this about?'

"Girls, girls, what is going on?" Mom asked.

"Mom, we missed you guys so much. You will have a hard time believing us when we tell you what hap-pened," Izzy answered.

"Well, I can try. So can you tell me now why you are home so early?" Mom questioned again.

"On this day, you and Dad went to the store and never came back. You were killed in a car accident. These magical girls named Anne and Amanda came to us and told us that we could travel in time to save you. We've been to so many different places! We've been trying so hard to get back to this moment in time to save you from going to the store," I said, struggling to hold back tears as I word vomited.

Again, our parents looked very confused and

peeked at each other to subtly communicate their skepticism.

"Now girls, this isn't something funny to joke about. Why are you actually home early?" Dad chimed in with a sly smile.

"We aren't joking. It all really happened. I know we must sound crazy. It is inexplicable, but we are telling the truth," Kate said. Our parents always believed Kate above all. She was the smartest child in the family and was not one to joke around.

Despite Kate's response, our parents still did not look convinced. But now, they looked even more confused because they knew that Kate was not one to ever lie or make up stories.

"What places have you been and how did you get there then?" Mom questioned.

"We traveled in what they called a Time Warp. It is a magical hole full of colors and it takes you to different places in time. We went far back in history to an old town, we traveled across ice to get off a deserted island, we went to a tropical beach for a week, and so many other places Mom!" I chimed in.

"Christal even turned into an elephant!" Izzy added, probably not helping our credibility.

My dad looked at my mom again with the telepathic communication that all parents seem to have.

"Well, honey, it is kind of weird that Christal immediately told us to be careful when she picked up the phone," Mom said. My dad just slowly nodded, pondering with his "science" brain how this could even be possible. He was probably thinking about next steps to get us tested for concussions at this point; I mean I did hit my head pretty hard on that pole.

"You were going to leave a message on the answering machine letting us know that you had picked up Lucy and would be grocery shopping, right?" I asked and my mom silently nodded. "We heard that message, but it cut out mid-way, and shortly after that Anne and Amanda showed up. They told us that you had been killed in an accident," I explained, "and that we could go back in time and stop it from happening!"

"I don't know if I will ever be able to believe this, girls. This is quite a story, just to get out of trouble for leaving school early," Mom paused and pondered. "You really didn't skip school?" Mom asked again.

"No, we swear!" we all said in some version or another. It was almost comedic considering how closely all our teachers watch us when we are at school. There really isn't a way to "skip" class at our age unless you just stay in the bathroom for half an hour.

"Hmm. Well, whatever happened, I guess we can't be mad, because it seems that you girls really do believe it," Mom said.

We had anticipated that our parents would be hard to convince. That's why we were careful to hold onto the magical book to show them, as well as our rings. Kate grabbed her backpack, where we'd stashed them for safekeeping. I watched her slowly unzip it and anxiously waited for her to pull out the book or rings, but instead she kept digging around with her eyes squinted and mouth in a slight frown.

"The book and rings are gone," Kate finally acknowledged, confirming my suspicion.

All she found was a note written on a tiny piece of loose-leaf paper. It read:

> *Yay! You did it. Congratulations sisters. We took the rings and book back for the next family that needs them. Plus, the unbelievable can never be explained. It can only be felt in your heart and remembered forever.*
> *Love,*
> *Anne and Amanda*

And with that, we knew that we may never be able to prove what happened. Our parents may never fully believe our story and know all that we went through to save them. But my sisters and I knew and would never forget; that would have to be enough...for now.

About the Author

Taylor Coblentz imagined the idea for this book when she was only 10 years old. The idea slowly came to life in this debut book throughout the course of many years. She currently teaches upper elementary students in Michigan and loves sharing her love of reading and writing. She hopes to write more books to share with students in her classroom and beyond.

www.ingramcontent.com/pod-product-compliance
Lightning Source LLC
Chambersburg PA
CBHW020732310726

48969CB00003B/802